For Daniel and Hubba·

Thanks Mahonri·

Library of Congress Control Number: 2014905402

Once in a misty rain forest, there was the Thunderbird. It helped to take care of the people who lived in the forest by making it rain. Thunderbird had a lot of work, and luckily there was help.

When Thunderbird made it rain in the Elk Valley, there was a Lightning Fish to help make the rain and lightning.

The Lightning Fish of Elk Valley was glad to be helpful and important, and would often brag to the Elk who lived in the Valley about how special being a Lightning Fish was.

The Elk grew tired of listening to how important Lightning Fish was. One day, an Elk from another valley was visiting and heard Lightning Fish talking about how special being the only Lightning Fish was.

The visiting Elk asked "But what about the other Lightning Fish? Aren't they special?"

Lightning Fish laughed at this, "There are no others like me."

But the Elk insisted, "We have a Lightning Fish in my Valley, the Good Water Valley. Thunderbird comes there too and they make it rain together."

Lightning Fish had never thought that there could be another Lightning Fish. Being not the only one made Lightning Fish feel not special, and not important. Lightning Fish did not like that.

Lightning Fish left the Elk Valley to go to the Good Water Valley to see if there was another Lightning Fish and if that Lightning Fish was special, helpful, and important.

Lightning Fish didn't stop to think about the Elk and the plants, how they weren't the only ones, but they were still special.

*W*hen the Lightning Fish from Elk Valley got to Good Water Valley, things looked beautiful, and that just made the Lightning Fish angry. So angry that Lightning Fish attacked the Other Lightning Fish without even a hello.

*T*hey fought so much, Thunderbird noticed, and came to see what was happening. Thunderbird called for the fighting to stop.

"*W*hy are you fighting? You're my helpers and my friends!"

Lightning Fish from Elk Valley thought it was all because of Thunderbird.

"I thought I was the only Lightning Fish! I was your special helper and your friend, and I was important, but I'm really not!"

"Just because I have other helpers, doesn't make you or your help unimportant. I want everyone in the forest to be a helper. It is home for all of us."

"I want to be the only special one, or I won't help anymore!"

"You can't make choices about someone else, only about you. You don't have to be my helper, but you can't be the only Lightning Fish."

But Lightning Fish from Elk Valley was still angry,

"Then I will keep fighting!"

"It makes me sad that you would choose that, but I won't let you hurt the Other Lightning Fish anymore."

Thunderbird placed Lightning Fish from Good Water Valley in a cave.

"The waters from this spring are magic, and will heal your hurt, but it will take a long time, so you will have to stay here until you are healed."

The Other Lightning Fish was sad to have to be in the cave to heal for a long time, and cried hot tears, turning the spring hot.

Thunderbird scooped up Lightning Fish from Elk Valley and flew back to Elk Valley. Lightning Fish was still angry and sad.

As Thunderbird was flying away Lightning Fish yelled

"Am I the most important?"

Thunderbird called back

"No one, not even me, is the most important."

Lightning Fish was so sad and angry at not feeling important anymore that Lightning Fish dug a hole deep down, and crawled in.

Lightning Fish decided to wait in the dark under the ground, until Thunderbird returned to say that Lightning Fish was the most important.

Lightning Fish cried hot tears instead of choosing to be part of the forest with everyone, making the hot spring of Elk Valley.

28036188R00018

Made in the USA
Charleston, SC
31 March 2014